But you promised!

BEL MOONEY

But you promised!

Illustrated by Margaret Chamberlain

mammoth

For Tom Woodward

First published in Great Britain 1994
by Methuen Children's Books Limited

This edition first published in 2001 by Mammoth
an imprint of Egmont Children's Books Limited
a division of Egmont Holding Limited
239 Kensington High Street, London W8 6SA
for The Book People Ltd
Hall Wood Avenue, Haydock, St Helens WA11 9UL

Text copyright © 1994 Bel Mooney
Illustrations copyright © 1994 Margaret Chamberlain

The moral rights of the author and illustrator have been asserted

ISBN 0 7497 2330 0

1 3 5 7 9 10 8 6 4 2

A CIP catalogue record for this title
is available from the British Library

Printed in Great Britain
by Cox & Wyman Ltd, Reading, Berkshire

Contents

But you promised!

. . . I could have a pet

'But you *promised* I could have a pet,' wailed Kitty.

'No I didn't,' said Mum firmly. 'Not a proper promise. I just said . . .'

'You said I could have a dog for Christmas – you DID!'

Kitty was cross and disappointed. Mum and Dad had said she could have a pet for Christmas, and she and Daniel had decided a dog would be most fun. But now Mum had a job, and so she said it would be too much trouble. 'I'll have so much to do, Kitty,' she sighed. 'You must understand.'

But Kitty only understood one thing. 'You *said* we'd get a dog, and Dad said he'd like one too, didn't you Dad?'

'Well, yes, I did,' said Dad.

'I want us to have a pet. All the boys in

school have animals. And I'd help Kitty look after it,' said Daniel.

'But puppies need training, and dogs have to be taken for walks, and dog food has to be bought – and who'd do all that?' asked Mum. 'I wanted this job so much, and it means I'll have less time to do all the things I have to do.'

'What about a little kitten?' asked Kitty, in a small voice.

'I don't want extra chores,' said Mum firmly. 'I'm sorry.' She sounded cross, but a bit guilty too.

Kitty looked furious.

Dan looked disappointed.

'Oh dear,' said Dad.

Kitty turned and ran from the room, not minding that she made all the decorations on the tree shiver as she passed. Up in her room she picked up Mr Tubs and hugged him. 'Grown-ups *never* keep their promises,' she whispered. 'So it looks as if we won't get our puppy, Mr T.'

She thought for a moment. 'Never mind, he might have tried to play with you and torn you by accident . . .'

Mr Tubs had lovely soft fur and a wonderful smell, and he always made Kitty feel better. If she was cross or sad or worried, all she had to do was pick up her favourite bear and squeeze him tightly, and soon she would think of a good game to play, and forget her troubles.

'You always give me ideas, Mr Tubs,' said Kitty slowly. It was happening now . . . the soft fur . . . the friendly brown eyes . . . Yes! Kitty had a brilliant plan.

She went to empty her money-box. There

wasn't much inside, because she had done most of her Christmas shopping. But there were still some coins left, and Kitty knew she could borrow some from Dad. And there were three more days until Christmas day . . .

On Christmas morning Daniel and Kitty opened their stockings early. It seemed a long wait until after breakfast, when they could have the presents under the tree. Lovely mysterious parcels in strange shapes . . . Kitty was so excited, she even forgot to be disappointed that there was nothing which yapped or miaowed.

At last it was present time. After they had opened a few gifts from aunts and uncles, Dan turned to Kitty with a grin and said, 'Here you are, Kit – open mine.'

It was small and squashy. Kitty pulled off all the paper in a rush – and there was a little, cuddly brown felt dog, with floppy ears.

'It's a pet for you, Kit,' said Dan.

Kitty couldn't believe it. She hugged her brother, then handed him her parcel. It was medium-sized and squashy. Daniel pulled off all the paper in a rush – and there was a cuddly black and white furry dog, with pointed ears and a pink felt tongue.

'It's a mascot for you, Dan – because you wanted a pet, too,' said Kitty.

'Help! We could open a pet shop,' smiled Dad. Then Mum handed him a parcel. It was

quite large, and squashy. Dad pulled off all the paper in a rush – and there was a big, grey, cuddly dog with hair all over its black glass eyes, and big paws.

'It's my little joke present, dear,' Mum said, 'because I decided you wanted a pet as much as the children did!'

Dad, Daniel and Kitty looked at each other, and at the three toy dogs – and then they laughed and laughed.

'Now,' said Mum. 'Open this, Kitty.' She handed Kitty a small white envelope.

On a piece of paper inside was this rhyme:

An empty bed, for friends to stay,
Is where you'll find a friend today

'That's easy,' said Kitty, 'It's the spare room. But what. . . ?'

Dad was smiling. 'Go and see,' he said.

Kitty ran upstairs, and they all followed her. She pushed open the spare-room door – and gasped. There, on the bed, was a large square cage, with an enormous ribbon wrapped round it, and a large label saying, 'Happy Christmas, Kitty, love from Mum and Dad.'

Inside was the tiniest, sweetest, prettiest baby hamster. She was honey-coloured, with bright eyes and neat little whiskers. When she heard them, she ran into her little house and peeped out nervously.

'Oh . . . oh . . . OH!' gasped Kitty. She was so pleased, she couldn't speak.

'What are you going to call her, Kit?' asked Daniel.

'Oh – I don't know. What about Sandy – 'cos she's that sort of colour?' Kitty said.

'That's a lovely name,' said Mum.

'But . . . but . . . why did you change your mind, Mum?' asked Kitty, running to hug her.

'I didn't change my mind, I just kept a promise,' said Mum.

'Anyway, hamsters are easy to look after,' said Dad. 'But you've got to promise to do it *properly*.'

Kitty opened the cage door, stretched out a hand, and stroked Sandy very gently on the nose with her finger. Who wouldn't keep a promise like that?

But you promised!

. . . You wouldn't be cross

It was one of those bad days. Kitty never knew how they began. Dad said it was because of getting out of bed the wrong side, but Kitty knew that was impossible. Her bed was up against the wall.

Whatever the reason, everything was going wrong. Kitty didn't want to do anything, and she lost things, and she thought that nothing seemed fair . . . but no matter how bad-tempered she got, Mum and Dad took no notice.

'What's wrong with Mum and Dad?' she asked her brother.

'They're in a good mood,' said Dan, 'but you wouldn't understand that, Kitty.'

'Why not?'

'Because you don't know what a good mood is!' He laughed, stuck out his tongue at her, and ran away.

Kitty was very, very cross. She chased her brother out of the kitchen, and along the hall. But he was too quick for her, and darted out through the front door.

'Stupid brothers!' said Kitty, and went into the living room, slamming the door behind her. And that was when it started . . .

Kitty slammed the door so hard it made the room shake, and a big old vase on the table by the door trembled, and fell over. It cracked into three big pieces – but worse than that, it

fell against Sandy's cage, which was right at the edge of the table.

Crash! – the cage fell to the ground. The little door flew open and a terrified hamster scuttled out, moving faster than Kitty had ever seen her move before. 'Stop, Sandy!' Kitty yelled, and dived down to try to catch her. Sandy slipped through her hands like a bar of wet soap – but Kitty knocked over the round table with all its little photographs in frames.

'Sandy!' Kitty cried, crawling on her hands and knees and seeing her pet disappear behind the sofa. In a panic she pulled all the cushions off, and piled them at the other end so Sandy could not get out. Then, puffing and blowing, she pulled the sofa away from the wall – knocking over the standard lamp. The standard lamp in turn knocked over a vase of flowers, and all the water poured on to Mum's new rug . . .

The room was a mess, but Kitty didn't notice. All she could think was that if Sandy went down a hole in the skirting board she would be lost forever.

But it was all right. She made a last grab, and held her hamster tightly in her hands. In a moment Sandy was back safely in her cage – and it was then Kitty looked around. And she heard Mum and Dad come in through the

kitchen door from the garden.

She was smiling sweetly when she went through the kitchen door. 'What's wrong?' asked Dad.

'You've had a change of mood,' said Mum.

'Mum and Dad, you know I think you're the best parents in the world?'

'Ye-es,' they said together, smiling.

'Well, if I tell you something, promise you won't be cross?'

'Oh, it's too nice a day to be bad-tempered,' laughed Dad, 'so what is it?'

'Sandy escaped, and I made a bit of a mess in the living room trying to catch her,' said Kitty.

'Oh, not to worry. What's a little mess?' said Mum, cheerfully.

But when they opened the living-room door and saw the chaos, Mum's face fell.

'Good heavens, Kitty, do you call this a LITTLE mess?' roared Dad, going very red.

'But you promised not to be cross,' said Kitty.

'We hadn't *seen* it then!' said Mum, staring around with horror. 'Oh, Kitty, when I get my hands on you . . .'

Kitty went backwards down the hall. 'But you said . . .'

'Never mind that,' said Dad. 'I'll tell you what. We won't be cross if you promise to do whatever we say.'

'Oh, yes,' said Kitty.

'Right, then,' he said, 'TIDY THE ROOM.'

'On my *own*?'

They nodded, looking stern.

Kitty groaned. 'But . . .'

' . . . You *promised*!' they both said.

But you promised!

. . . It wouldn't hurt

Kitty was hiding. She could hear Mum calling her, and Dad telling Dan to look in the toy cupboard. But she stuffed her fingers in her ears and closed her eyes, and wished, wished, *wished* that they would all go away.

'KITTY!' called Mum.

'NO – I won't, I won't,' whispered Kitty to herself.

The trouble was this. Kitty had to go to the doctor to have an injection, and she didn't want to go. So while the family was having breakfast she crept under the pretty cloth that covered a little round table on the landing – right to the ground. It was such an obvious place to hide that Mum, Dad and Dan rushed past it, looking for her.

At last she heard Mum say that she had to go to work, and Dan say he had to go to school.

Dad had taken time off work to go with Kitty – and so now she held her breath, and closed her eyes, waiting for him to find her.

He stood by the table. She could see his feet. 'Now, where can my naughty girl be . . .?' he said to himself. There was a pause.

Then Kitty opened her eyes – to see Dad's face peering under the cloth at her. 'Come on out, Kit!' he grinned.

Five minutes later she was sitting at the kitchen table, while Dad made her some toast. 'Oh, Dad, I don't want to go to the doctor's,' she wailed.

'Why not?' he asked.

'Because it's an injection, and I hate them. I hate needles going into me.'

'But they do it so's you won't get really ill later,' said Dad, 'It's a good thing.'

'I don't care, I hate them,' scowled Kitty. 'And it will hurt. So I'm *not* going!'

'Yes, you are,' said Dad, pulling her to her feet, 'because it's important and, anyway, it won't hurt – I promise you.'

'Are you sure?' asked Kitty.

Dad nodded.

It seemed such a long time in the waiting room. Kitty tried to look at an Annual, but the pages were torn. And a baby was screaming on its mother's knees, and she couldn't concentrate – and she felt SO nervous.

At last they were called. Dad held her hand and they walked into the surgery. Dr Scott smiled at them, but Kitty didn't smile back. She knew the doctor was a jolly, kind lady who always gave children a sweet from the jar on her desk. She knew that it was important to have injections. But still she didn't smile.

'Oh, what a gloomy face,' smiled Dr Scott.

'I told her it won't hurt,' said Dad.

'Of course it won't,' said Dr Scott. 'Now just roll up your sleeve, Kitty. We'll just wipe the place to make it clean, like *that*, and you'll

feel a little tiny prick, like *that* . . .'

'OWW!' yelled Kitty.

She didn't cry – of course not. But she rubbed her arm, glared at Dr Scott and at Dad, and her mouth turned down at the corners. Dr Scott gave her a sweet and patted her on the head, saying she was a good girl – but Kitty was not happy.

When they got home, Dad made them a cup of tea. 'We'd better be quick, love. You've already missed half the morning's school. And I've got to get to work,' he said.

Kitty looked at him without smiling. 'It's

not fair, Dad,' she said. 'You said it wouldn't hurt, and it *did* hurt.'

'Oh, Kit, it didn't hurt very much,' he said.

'How do you know? You weren't inside my arm!' she replied. 'Anyway, you promised me it wouldn't hurt.'

Dad sat down at the table and sipped his tea, looking at her kindly. Then he put the mug down and shook his head. 'Now, Kit,' he said. 'You *know* parents aren't in charge of everything! There's a lot of things we can't control – like whether people are nice to you at school, or whether it will rain on sports day, or whether you'll hurt a little bit at the doctor or the dentist. You know that, don't you?'

'Well you shouldn't have promised,' said Kitty sternly.

Dad hugged her so hard she had to smile. 'Oh, Kit-Kat,' he said. 'One thing you'll have to learn – when grown-ups say "I promise" they usually mean "I hope"!'

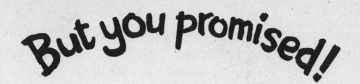

. . . I could stay the night

There was a craze at Kitty's school for staying the night with friends, but Kitty had never done it. Nobody had asked her. Daniel said it was because all the mums had heard how naughty she was. Kitty didn't think that was funny.

'*You* have to arrange it, Mum,' she said. 'You ring up Jane's mother, or Kate's, and then they ask me to stay the night.'

'All right, dear,' her Mum said, in that voice which sounds as if it is thinking of something else. 'We'll see.'

'Oh *why* do grown-ups always say that?' Kitty asked.

'All right, I promise you I'll arrange something – will that do?'

'Huh,' was all Kitty said.

Three days later it was Friday. The end of

the week always made Kitty feel cheerful. She was collected from school by William's mother, and she and William were planning to have a great game involving their two gardens – when Kitty stopped dead in the street.

'Oh, no!' she said, staring at the car outside her house. It was Aunty Susan's car – and that meant one thing. Melissa.

'Quick – run into our garden, and then they won't see you,' hissed William. He knew all about Kitty's cousin. But it was too late.

Kitty's Mum was beckoning from the window. So Kitty had to say goodbye to William and walk up her own path.

'Isn't this a lovely surprise?' said Kitty's Mum, gaily. 'Aunty Susan and Melissa have popped in for tea.'

'Uh,' said Kitty, chewing her fingers.

'Gosh, aren't your nails dirty?' said Melissa.

'Uh,' said Kitty.

'Kitty, can't you talk properly?' said her Mum.

'Nuh,' said Kitty.

'*Kitty*!' said Mum.

Aunty Susan took no notice. She was used to Kitty, and just ruffled her hair, making it messier than ever. (Melissa's hair was in two tight plaits, with pink and white checked ribbons.) 'Anyway, Kitty, before you came home, we made a lovely plan. You're coming back with us to stay the night!'

Kitty gulped. 'Tonight?'

Mum and Aunty Susan nodded.

'There you are, Kit,' Mum said. 'I've been promising you could stay the night with someone, and thanks to Aunty Susan we've got it organised.'

Kitty knew that when Mum spoke in that bright, loud voice there was no point in arguing.

It only took a few minutes for Mum to run upstairs and pack Kitty's bag – while Kitty sat nibbling a biscuit and feeling gloomy. Melissa beamed at her. 'Aren't you going to comb your hair before we go?' she asked.

Melissa's house was like Melissa – everything in place, everything very *nice*, but nothing inviting you to play and have a really good time. *Just* like Melissa.

All Kitty's cousin wanted to do was watch television – which Kitty thought boring. Or play with dolls – which Kitty thought even

more boring. She thought longingly of William's wild garden next door, and the amazing adventurous games they made up.

'It's time for bed,' said Aunty Susan. Kitty looked at the clock. She couldn't believe it.

'But it's Friday,' she said.

'Never mind, dear, girls still need their beauty sleep,' said Aunty Susan, kindly.

'*Yuk*,' thought Kitty.

She couldn't say 'No' because she was a guest – and she knew that guests don't argue. So Kitty trailed upstairs after Melissa, and was forced to have a bath. 'I like lots of scented bubbles in my baths,' said Melissa.

So Kitty allowed herself to be scrubbed, and her hair to be washed, and her nails cut – just like Melissa. They were wrapped in clean white towels. Then the hairdryer roared at them both, and Aunty Susan got busy with the brush – until at last Kitty hardly recognized herself in the mirror.

'Where's your nightie, Kitty?'

Kitty pulled on Dan's old pyjamas, with the picture of Superman on the front, and Melissa looked at her scornfully. *She* was wearing a long white nightdress with lacy frills. Kitty thought she looked like a ghost, and wanted to giggle. Then – 'Oh, NO!' cried Kitty.

31

'What?', said Melissa and her Mum together.

'Mum forgot to put Mr Tubs in my bag. I can't sleep without him.'

'Never mind, dear, here's one of Melissa's lovely dolls for you to cuddle,' said Aunty Susan, tucking Kitty into bed.

She put a story tape on for them to listen to – but Kitty thought it was babyish. She preferred reading, or talking. She lay uncomfortably next to the blonde doll with hard arms and legs, staring blue eyes, and fancy clothes which tickled. 'I *hate* you, doll,' she whispered, giving it a shove under the bedclothes.

Kitty missed home. She thought of her own messy bedroom, in her own cosy house, and of Mr Tubs, and of the fun of Saturday mornings when she and Dan and the children next door all played together . . .

'Mum?' she said inside her head. 'Can you hear me? I never want to stay the night away – not ever again!'

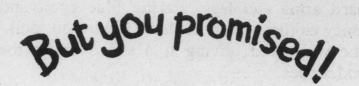

But you promised!

. . . You wouldn't tell

Dad was going to be in charge. It happened a lot nowadays, because Kitty's Mum's new job meant that sometimes she had to work on Saturdays. Once they got used to it, Kitty and Daniel didn't mind. They always had fun with Dad.

This Saturday morning, Mum was in a bossy mood. 'There's plenty of salad in the fridge for lunch,' she said, 'and I want you to eat it up.'

The children groaned.

'Rabbit food,' said Daniel.

'I don't want to eat silly, slimy salad,' said Kitty.

'Can't we have something else?' they moaned.

But Mum had become very keen on really healthy eating and insisted, 'It's *good* for you

34

all – but if you want something hot to go with it, Dad can cook you some rice. But remember, NO biscuits for elevenses. They're bad for your teeth.'

They groaned even more loudly. But Mum took no notice, just grabbed her coat, and left.

Dad shrugged. 'Better do as we're told, kids.'

Kitty stuck out her teeth, held two fingers above her head like ears and hopped around. 'I'll turn into a bunny if I eat any more lettuce, Dad!' she said.

He laughed, and sent them out into the garden to play while he did the washing up.

The morning passed quickly. Daniel and Kitty played hide-and-seek with William and Sally, the children next door, until heavy clouds made the sky dark. Kitty shivered.

'It's going to rain,' said Sally. 'Come in for a snack.'

Her mother gave them a plate of chocolate biscuits to share, and glasses of lemonade. Daniel winked at Kitty.

As lunch-time came near they decided they should go home. It had stopped raining, but the air was damp and cold. 'Lovely weather for salad,' Kitty groaned.

They were surprised to see a strange man sitting at the kitchen table with Dad. They each had a glass of beer. Dad looked very pleased. He told the children this was a very old friend he hadn't seen for years. The man, whose name was Bill, was big and jolly. He looked at his watch, 'Well, if your lady-wife isn't coming home, why don't we all go down the road and get fish and chips?'

The children jumped up and down,

screaming with delight, and clapping their hands.

Dad looked at them, then at the fridge door, then at his watch. 'We-ell . . .'

'Oh, come on!' said Bill.

'You'd better promise not to tell your Mum,' said Dad.

'We won't!' yelled Kitty.

Twenty minutes later they were all walking down the road, munching delicious fish and chips with their fingers. When they got back to the house Bill took cans of fizzy drink from his pockets, which made a perfect end to the meal. The children were sorry when he had to go.

'Oh, dear,' said Dad, looking at the mess of greasy newspaper and empty cans on the kitchen table. 'We'd better clear up. Mum will be back in half an hour.'

When Mum's key turned in the lock, Dad and Daniel were watching a film on television, and Kitty was wheeling Mr Tubs up and down the hall on her old baby tricycle.

Mum kissed her. 'Hello, love, have you had a lovely day?'

Kitty nodded. She started to feel a bit guilty.

'And it wasn't *so* bad to have salad for lunch, was it?' asked Mum.

Kitty looked at her and went red. It was no good. She couldn't tell fibs – that would be terrible. So she told Mum what had happened.

'Aha – he did, did he?' said Mum, folding her arms, a little smile curling at the corner of her mouth. She marched into the sitting room.

'Well, was it good, having a salad of fish and chips?' she asked, standing in between Dad and the TV.

Dad looked really guilty. He glanced sideways at Kitty, and she could almost hear him thinking, *'But you promised you wouldn't tell.'*

'Don't be cross with Dad,' she said.

At that, a big grin broke across Mum's face. 'Look at you all!' she said. 'Like frightened rabbits! You obviously *have* been eating too many greens. Well, if you must know I went to the market to get a special treat for tonight's supper, and I met Bill – which was a lovely surprise. And he told me about your lunch.'

'And you don't mind?' asked Dad.

'Course not. I'm not a witch, you know! Didn't I say I'm making something you like for supper?'

'What is it, Mum?' asked Kitty.

'Fish and chips!' said Mum.

'Oh, no!' they all groaned. And then they started to laugh.

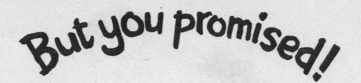

... *You'd choose me*

There was a new girl in Kitty's class. She was called Rosie, and she was very nice. On her first day she was put next to Kitty, who had to show her where everything was – they quickly became friends.

Rosie had short black curly hair, and laughed a lot. Very soon the teacher discovered that she was clever in lessons, as well as good at games.

'Oh, Rosie, you're so lucky,' Kitty sighed one day, 'because you're good at everything!'

'It's not *luck*,' Rosie said with a grin. 'It's hard work!'

Rosie and Kitty did everything together. They shared their biscuits at break, swapped books they liked, and chose each other as partners in gym and dancing.

'Will you always choose me, Rosie?' Kitty

asked – rather proud because her friend was better than all the rest.

'Course I will, silly.'

'Promise?'

'Cross my heart.'

Kitty was happy. She had always wanted a really *best* friend. It didn't matter that Rosie was a faster runner, or could dive like a fish.

They were friends. And that was more important than anything.

Or so Kitty thought – until the week before Sports Day.

Kitty didn't like Sports Day because, she said to Mum, 'It's no fun running a race and seeing all the others in front of you.'

'What does it matter – as long as you do your best?' asked Mum.

'Huh – my best isn't good enough,' growled Kitty.

Now the class was practising for all the events. Kitty watched Rosie come in first in the running race, and the long jump, and the high jump, and the sack race, too. She beat all the boys. Kitty felt so pleased.

They sat cross-legged in a group around the teacher, who said, 'Now children, I want you to choose partners for the three-legged race. So when I call your name, stand up, choose your partner and line up.'

After a minute she called out Rosie's name. Kitty sat up straight, and smiled. But Rosie wasn't looking at her. 'Er . . . Tom!' she said, excitedly.

Kitty felt as if the smile was glued to her face. She wouldn't let anyone see how hurt she was. But inside she felt like a crumpled ball of paper.

'It's all right, Kitty, you can be *my* partner,' whispered William.

Tom was tall, and very good at all sports. Of course he and Rosie finished first, giggling as they jogged over the line in front of all the other pairs. Kitty and William did quite well. At least they didn't fall over.

But Kitty felt strange inside. She was sad but she was angry too. It was a funny mixture.

At lunch-time Rosie came and sat next to her as usual, and opened her lunch box.

'You're very quiet, Kitty,' she said.

'Well, what do you expect,' said Kitty, in

her crossest voice, 'when you don't want to be my friend any more?'

Rosie looked surprised, so Kitty explained. 'And you promised I would always be your partner,' she ended.

'Did I?' asked Rosie, frowning.

Kitty nodded.

'But, Kitty, the thing is, I wanted . . . oh, I wanted to *win*, you see. And because I'm taller than you . . . well, we couldn't run together. It wouldn't work.'

'And you think winning is more important than being friends?' Kitty demanded.

Rosie shook her head. 'No. They're different, that's all. You're brilliant at art, and if there was a competition where you had to do a picture with a partner, you wouldn't want *me*. I'm hopeless at it, and you know that, don't you?'

Kitty said nothing. She hadn't thought of that. Rosie offered her a crisp.

'The IMPORTANT thing is, Kit – a friend is someone you choose to *talk* to. So now will you stop being so quiet? It doesn't suit you!'

Kitty felt suddenly happy. 'OK, Rosie,' she said.

But you promised!

. . . He'd get better

William's cat was very very old. At least, he wasn't really William's cat. His parents had bought Copper before Sally was born, so he was really a family pet. But it was William who fed him. And William loved him most of all.

One day Kitty went next door to find William looking sad and worried. Copper was ill. Very ill. His orangey-brown fur wasn't sleek and shiny any more, and he just lay in his basket not wanting to do anything. He even left his favourite cat food on the plate.

'What's the matter with him?' asked Kitty.

'We don't know,' said William, 'but he's never been like this before, have you, old thing?' And he stroked Copper gently.

William and Kitty went to William's Mum, who sat with Sally in the kitchen. 'Mum, what are we going to do about Copper?' asked

William, and to Kitty's surprise he sounded as if he was going to cry. She didn't blame him. She felt worried, too.

'I'm sure he'll get better, Will,' said Sally.

'Of course, he will!', said their mother.

'Are you sure?' asked William.

'Of course!' said his Mum.

'Promise?' said William.

'Yes, darling.'

When Kitty heard *that* she had a funny feeling . . . but William looked more cheerful. He went to tuck an old blanket over Copper, then he and Kitty played outside.

In the morning, when Kitty and her Mum collected him to walk to school, William looked miserable again. Copper was worse.

'Don't worry, love, I'll take him to the vet today,' said his mother.

At break Kitty and William talked about Copper. At lunch-time Kitty sat with William instead of Rosie, and they wondered how he was. When it came to going-home time, Kitty's mother had to stop them both running at full speed to find out.

They ran round to William's back door and pushed it open. His Mum sat at the kitchen table, and jumped when they rushed in. Her face was pale and sad. 'MUM! How's Copp. . . ?' William began.

'Oh, William, I'm so sorry . . . it's so sad . . . I took Copper to the vet's, and . . .

and . . . he isn't alive,' said William's Mum. This time *she* sounded as if she was going to cry.

'But why. . . ?' said William, in a small voice.

'He was too ill and too old. The vet had to put him to sleep. It didn't hurt him, Will.'

William stamped his foot. 'But you promised me he'd get better, Mum! YOU PROMISED!' he shouted, and then ran out of the room, slamming the door.

Kitty started to follow him, but his mother shook her head, looking very sad. 'Leave him, Kitty,' she said.

At home, Kitty sat down in the sitting room, without saying a word. Daniel was watching television. The chattering noise irritated Kitty. Suddenly she jumped up, and switched it off. 'Hey!' protested Daniel, then stopped – because Kitty burst into tears.

Dan fetched Mum, and when Mum had put Kitty on her knee and hugged her and wiped her eyes, Kitty explained why she was upset.

'*Why* do animals have to die, Mum?' she whispered, looking across the room to where Sandy scampered around her cage.

'Because . . .'

'Because what?'

'Because they just do. And so do we. We

just live longer,' said Mum, holding Kitty close.

'William's Mum shouldn't have made that promise, then,' said Kitty. And she explained what his mother had said.

'Oh, but, Kitty, remember what Dad always says?' said Mum.

'When grown-ups say "*I promise*", they usually mean "*I hope*",' said Kitty.

'Exactly,' said Mum.

Next day, in school, William was very quiet. At break he sat with Kitty in a corner, and they talked about Copper again. Kitty wanted him to feel better. 'You know, Will, Copper's probably having a lovely time in Heaven,' she said.

William looked at her. His eyes lit up. 'Promise me that's true!' he said.

Kitty said nothing for a few seconds. Then she smiled at him – feeling very grown-up all of a sudden – and said, 'I can't do that, Will – but let's just say, I *hope*.'

But you promised!

. . . We'd go out

It was a lovely, hot summer Saturday. Kitty and Daniel wanted to go to the park. Mum had said she would take them. She had *promised* they would go out.

But now she sat at the desk in the corner of the sitting room, doing sums on her calculator. 'I have to get this done, kids,' she said.

'Oh, WHY do grown-ups always break their promises?' said Daniel.

'Because they say "I promise" just to keep us quiet,' growled Kitty.

'Honestly, you two! You've jolly well got to understand that this is part of my new job, and I have to do it this morning,' said Mum. 'The thing about being grown-up is – things can't be all play.'

'Well I don't want to be a grown-up, I can promise you that!' muttered Kitty, cradling

Sandy in her hands and thinking it was more fun being a hamster than a child.

William's mother had arranged to take them swimming in the afternoon, and they had a marvellous time. But when they got home they heard Mum and Dad arguing.

'You just forgot!' said Mum.

'I've been really busy,' said Dad.

'But you PROMISED we'd go out!' said Mum, sounding really cross and very upset at the same time.

'I know I did,' said Dad, unhappily. 'But it's too late to get a babysitter now.'

'You forgot our anniversary last year, too,' said Mum.

'I didn't exactly forget this year . . . I just forgot to organise a babysitter,' said Dad.

'Huh. And last year you made a *solemn promise* you'd take me out for a marvellous dinner,' sniffed Mum.

Daniel looked at Kitty, and Kitty looked at Daniel. 'Quick,' she hissed. 'We've got to think of a plan.' Mum and Dad sat in the sitting room not speaking to each other. And Kitty and Daniel crept into the kitchen and whispered . . .

Twenty minutes later Kitty went to the sitting room and called them. 'Come and see what we've done!' she said.

Surprised, but still looking cross with each other, Mum and Dad got up and followed her through the kitchen into the back garden. Then they stood and stared.

Daniel had set up the garden table, and Kitty had covered it with a pretty cloth. They had set two places with the best knives and forks and china, and put a sparkling wine glass at each place.

Dan had found a dusty bottle of wine, a present from some visitors, and Kitty had picked ten fine roses, for the number of years

Mum and Dad had been married. They had lit a candle in the middle of the table (even though it was still light), and moved the radio to the kitchen windowsill, so that romantic music drifted into the garden . . .

'There you are!' said Kitty. 'Now all Dad has to do is drive down to that Greek restaurant you like and get a takeaway!'

'And we're the waiters,' added Dan.

Mum's eyes shone all bright and damp – and she ran to hug them both. Then Dad put out

an arm, and gave *her* a really huge cuddle.

'Was this your idea all along, dear?' said Mum softly, smiling at him.

'I'm not going to let myself off the hook that easily,' said Dad. 'No, it was their idea. I didn't put them up to it. I'm just lucky I've got two brilliant children!'

'It was Kit's idea really,' said Dan. 'She said that "out" could mean the garden!'

'Yes,' said Kitty wickedly. 'I just wanted to prove to you both that promises CAN be kept!'

Also by Bel Mooney

I DON'T WANT TO!

Kitty's favourite word is NO! She
doesn't want to clean her teeth or wash
or eat her vegetables or – worst of all –
play with boring cousin Melissa. But
saying no gives Kitty more problems
than even *she* bargained for – and
somehow she always ends up wanting to
say yes!

I CAN'T FIND IT!

Kitty was always losing things. She wasn't careless, but things she put away very, very carefully just – sort of – moved, all by themselves . . . Then one day, Kitty finds something no one else can find.

This is the hilarious and touching sequel to **I DON'T WANT TO!**

IT'S NOT FAIR!

Kitty is puzzled. Why is she the shortest in
her class?
Why can't anyone in her family take a joke?
Why can't she go to bed as late as her
older brother?
Why don't holidays last forever? Why aren't
things fair?
One day Mum says it too and Kitty comes up
with a fantastic idea . . .

Bel Mooney has made sure that Kitty, the very
popular heroine of I DON'T WANT TO! and
I CAN'T FIND IT! is as irrepressible and
lovable as ever . . .

I KNOW!

Kitty decides as she gets older that she *knows* things. The trouble is, grown-ups keep treating her like a baby. So Kitty sets out to show just how much she knows – and gets one or two surprises, including a very special Easter!

Tony Bradman

DILLY THE DINOSAUR

Dilly is the naughtiest dinosaur in the whole world.

There was the time he decided he wasn't ever going to wash again. Another day he decorated his bedroom using his sister's best painting set.

And when he *doesn't* get his way, he opens his mouth and lets loose his ultra-special, 150-mile-per-hour super-scream!

Other DILLY titles are

Dilly's Muddy Day
Dilly Tells the Truth
Dilly & the Tiger
Dilly & the Ghost
Dilly Dinosaur, Superstar
Dilly the Angel
Dilly and the Big Kids
Dilly Goes on Holiday